HALLOWEEN MOTEL

HALLOWEEN MOTEL

BY **SEAN** "SCREAM INSIDE THE HOUSE" **DIVINY**
ILLUSTRATED BY **JOE** "THE REVENGE OF THE . . ." **ROCCO**

SCHOLASTIC INC.
New York Toronto London Auckland Sydney
Mexico City New Delhi Hong Kong Buenos Aires

ISBN 0-439-33294-X

Text copyright © 2000 by Sean Diviny.
Illustrations copyright © 2000 by Joe Rocco. All rights reserved. Published by
Scholastic Inc.,
555 Broadway, New York, NY 10012, by arrangement with
Joanna Cotler Ghouls,
a Screamprint of HarperCollins Publishers.
SCHOLASTIC and associated logos are trademarks
and/or registered trademarks of Scholastic Inc.

12 11 10 9 8 7 6 5 4 3 2 1   1 2 3 4 5 6/0

Printed in the U.S.A.   24

First Scholastic printing, October 2001

Typography and cover design by Alicia "I Married a Monsterrobot" Mikles

The broken buzzing neon sign had letters falling off.
The fog was thick and cold and damp. It gave my dad a cough!

The pool had something swimming in it—
really **long** and weird!
A sign read, "Swim at your own risk.
The lifeguard disappeared."

The coffee shop had waitresses so pale it made me shiver.
Scarier than that though was the nightly special—**LIVER!**
"You look hungry, dear," they said.
"Come in here for a **BITE**.
We'll be here until the dawn.
Come *VISIT US* tonight!"

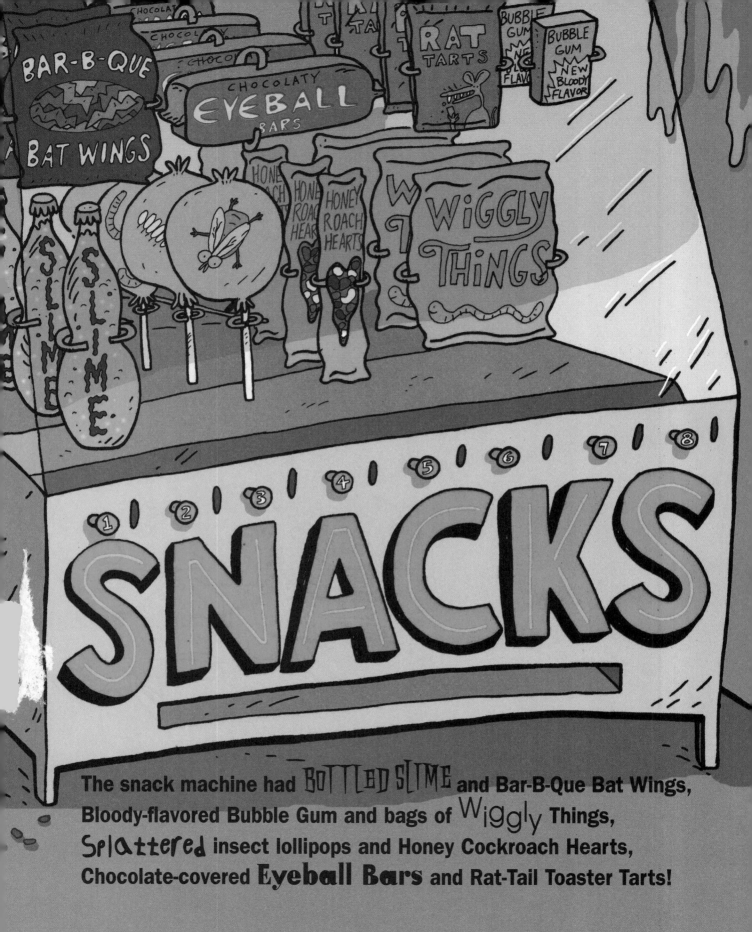

The snack machine had BOTTLED SLIME and Bar-B-Que Bat Wings,
Bloody-flavored Bubble Gum and bags of Wiggly Things,
Splattered insect lollipops and Honey Cockroach Hearts,
Chocolate-covered Eyeball Bars and Rat-Tail Toaster Tarts!

Halloween Motel. Oh, no!
They've got a vacancy.
Heed my warning. Don't you go!
Oh, turn around and flee!

The bed was kind of creepy with a tombstone at the head.
The phone looked like a skull and bone. I tried it. It was dead!
The TV turned on by itself and showed a horror flick.
The furniture had feet and claws that gave my mom a kick!

The bellman brought our luggage up.
His face was sort of hairy.
His eyes were **gooey yellow**,
and his BREATH was really scary!
My dad tipped him a quarter,
and he bared his teeth and **GROWLED**.
My mom gave him a dollar more,
and, joyfully, he howled!

"Now, let's see," my dad said
as he studied the brochure.
"Trick-or-treating starts at dusk.
Let's KNOCK on every door!"

My dad dressed up as Elvis. My mom was a baboon.
And I was Captain Muscle from that wrestling cartoon.
A **FULL MOON** rose behind us, and the motel seemed to glow.
"Time to trick-or-treat," said Mom. "C'mon, you two. Let's go!"

Vampires in
Room Seventeen
threw apples
that were
CHEWED!

Room Ten's *Ghostly Lady* only stared at us and **booed!**

A **stinky**
BIGFOOT
MONSTER

in Room Eight
gave me
his soap.

An *Evil Scientist* next door d r o p p e d in a micro**scope.**

The Aliens in Room Fourteen tossed out a **globe** and **map**!

The **Z**ombies in Room Six just growled, "We're *trying* to take a nap!"